Sunday Shopping

story by Sally Derby

pictures by Shadra Strickland

Lee & Low Books Inc. * New York

LEE & LOW BOOKS Inc., 95 Madison Avenue, New York, NY 10016, leeandlow.com
Book design by David and Susan Neuhaus/NeuStudio
Book production by The Kids at Our House
The text is set in Venis
The illustrations are rendered in a mix of watercolor, acrylic, and wax pencil and then digitally composed
Manufactured in China by Nordica International Ltd., March 2015
10 9 8 7 6 5 4 3 2 1
First Edition

Library of Congress Cataloging-in-Publication Data
Derby, Sally.
Sunday shopping / story by Sally Derby ; pictures by Shadra Strickland. — First edition.
pages cm
Summary: "Every Sunday night a young girl and her grandmother go on an imaginary shopping trip using play
money and the advertisements in the newspaper as a guide for their 'purchases.'" —Provided by publisher.
ISBN 978-1-60060-438-6 (hardcover : alk. paper)
[1. Shopping—Fiction. 2. Grandmothers—Fiction. 3. Imagination—Fiction.] I. Strickland, Shadra, illustrator. II. Title.
PZ7.D4416Sun 2014   [E]—dc23   2013047488

For all grandmas, especially
Grandma Chester—S.D.

To Pat Cummings.
Thank you—S.S.

On Sunday night, after we put on our nightgowns,
Grandma and I go shopping.

Grandma wears her blue hat
with the feather that's only a little bent.

I hold her big black purse
with our shopping money inside.

I get my scissors and tape ready,
and Grandma opens the newspaper.

Look here, Evie," Grandma says. "Hook's Grocery is having a sale, and I've got a taste for ham. Think I'll buy us a big chunk and cook it up with some beans."

"Ham's good how you cook it," I tell her, and I feel my tummy rumble.

"If you buy some extra, we can have it for breakfast too."

"Good idea," Grandma says. "I'll get a *really* big chunk, and we'll eat ham all week. Ham and sweet potatoes, ham salad, . . .

"Maybe ham sandwiches one day? With yellow mustard?" I ask.

Grandma nods. "Why not? Paper says rye bread is two for a dollar forty-nine. We'll buy two loaves and give one to Sophie Green downstairs. Pay the cashier, Evie."

I pull out a twenty. Our shopping dollars are easy to tell apart because they're all different colors.

"Keep the change," I say, just like they do on TV.

"Where we going next?" I ask.
Grandma turns the page.

"My stars!" she says. "Listen to this.
Hill's Furniture is closing. 'Everything Must Go.'

"Look at this fine furniture. Let's buy a roomful.
You want to choose first, honey?" Grandma asks.

"Can I pick two things, Grandma?"
"Pick all you like," she tells me.

I choose the Sofa with a Secret. It comes with two squishy pillows, and the secret is that you can open it up into a big bed at night. I bet it won't have any lumpy spots either.

"Do we have room for the Giant TV and the Sofa with a Secret both, Grandma?" I ask.

"We'll make room," she says.

"Now it's your turn," I tell Grandma, and she shows me a fluffy rug.

"Mmmm, mmmm! Winter mornings, with a thick rug to step down on, feet won't mind getting up. What color you want, Evie? It don't come in purple."

Grandma's teasing, 'cause she knows purple's my favorite color.

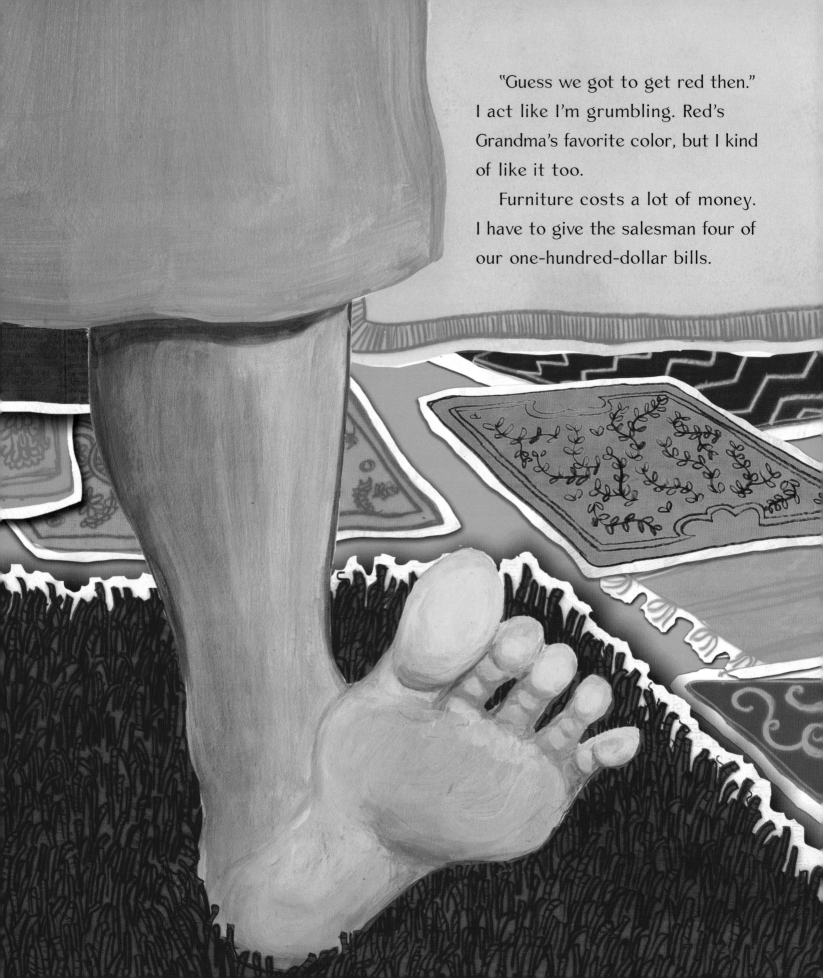

"Guess we got to get red then."
I act like I'm grumbling. Red's
Grandma's favorite color, but I kind
of like it too.

Furniture costs a lot of money.
I have to give the salesman four of
our one-hundred-dollar bills.

Next door to Hill's is Pace Jewels and Treasures.

"Can we go to Pace's, Grandma, just this once?" I ask. "If we get this little jewelry box, I could keep my necklace in it."

Mama gave me my necklace the day she left for the army, and I only take it off at night. It has a real gold heart on a chain, and inside the heart is a picture of Mama on one side and Grandma on the other. We've got a picture of Mama on the table by Grandma's bed, but the heart picture stays with me wherever I go.

Grandma says yes, we can go in. This time she has to pay the money because I don't want to let go of my beautiful new box.

Grandma turns the page. "Oh my!" she says. "See what it says here, honey. 'New for Spring.' Look at all these fancy clothes."

She's looking at two whole pages of ladies and girls smiling big smiles and with their hair fixed just so.

"Here's where we should get you some new clothes," Grandma tells me.
"And some for you too," I say.

"I'm not the one outgrowing everything!"
Grandma's laugh chuckles up till her tummy shakes the paper.

I choose a pink-and-white skirt, a fuzzy sweater, purple tights, and purple barrettes for my hair. That's what I'll wear when I win the gold trophy for Best Second-Grade Speller in Ohio. I'm already the best second-grade speller in my school. I won when I spelled *scissors* right, after Curtis Williams left out the *c*.

I get socks, and sneakers like the older kids wear. I pick out a beautiful yellow swimsuit too.

"It's not summer yet, Evie," Grandma says. She's right, so I put the swimsuit back and buy a dress with shiny spangles for Grandma instead. Then I pay the saleslady with our last one hundred.

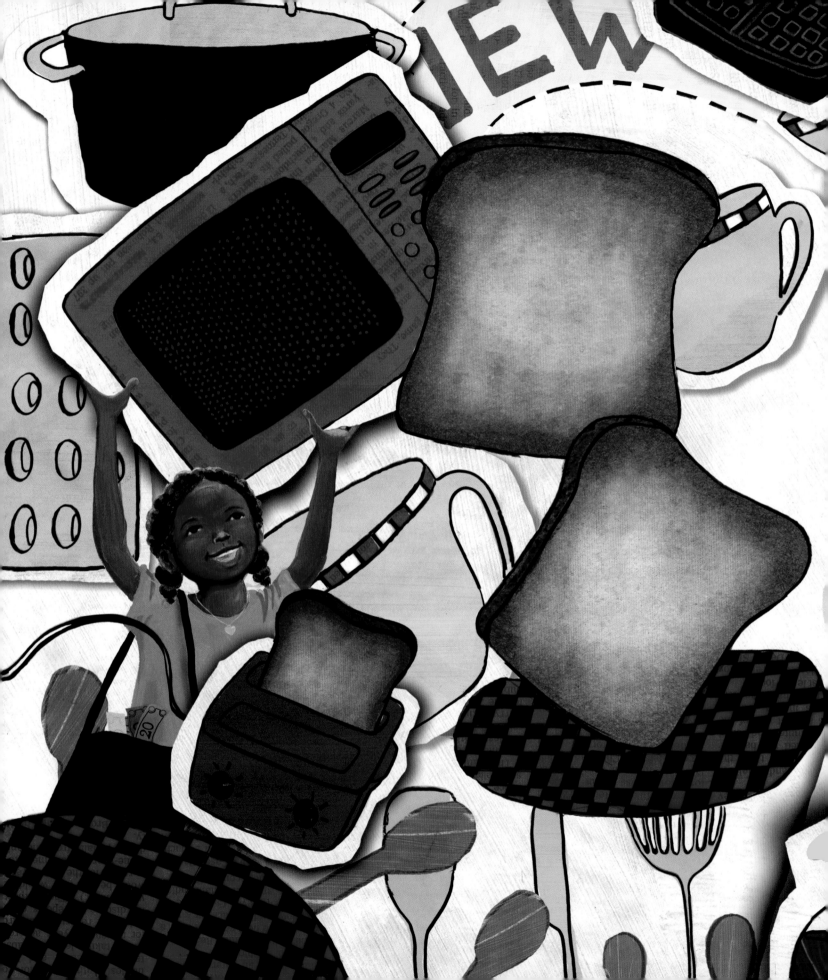

Next we go to Hank's Home Hardware. I choose a Super-Improved Microwave Oven with a special popcorn setting and a shiny toaster that pops the toast up by itself like ours used to do. Then Grandma chooses a coffeemaker with a little clock timer so she can put coffee and water in at night, and the coffee will be ready right when she gets up in the morning.

How much money we got left?" Grandma asks after I pay for our kitchen things.

My fingers scramble around in the purse. I pull out a fifty and a twenty.

"Enough," I say. So we stop in the All-U-Need. I buy a chocolate bar, a Three-Ring Notebook with Five Dividers for school, and popcorn for our new microwave. Grandma gets Salon Shampoo for Glorious Hair and Brite Toothpaste for a Beautiful Smile.

"'Bout time to go home, Evie," Grandma says when we're leaving the All-U-Need. "Stores will be closing soon."

"I need to buy one more thing," I tell her. "But you can't look."

"I won't," she promises. She turns away and covers her eyes with her hands.

I go to Florence's Flower Shoppe. I get the Sunday Special—a bunch of beautiful red and white tulips—and I hide them under my pillow.

Now we're both tired, so I put away the scissors and tape.
I curl up my necklace on my new jewelry box.

Grandma closes her purse, takes off her hat,
and folds the newspaper nice so the scraps don't hang out.

I snuggle under my covers, and Grandma kisses me good night. Then she gets into her bed and turns out the light.

I listen until I hear her breathing slow and easy. Then I tiptoe over and lay the tulips next to Mama's picture for Grandma to find in the morning.

Our shopping dollars are all gone, but we don't mind. On Friday we'll pretend that a famous movie star comes driving down our street. He stops out front and says he lived in this very building when he was a little boy. Then photographers will take pictures of him giving away bags full of money.

And next Sunday night we'll go shopping again.